Meatloaf Monster from the School Cafeteria

Originally published as
*Cream of Creature from
the School Cafeteria*

by Mike Thaler
Illustrated by Jared Lee

SCHOLASTIC INC.

For Joe Belperio—
We will miss you.
—M.T.

Meatloaf Monster first appeared as *Cream of Creature* in 1985.
With a revised title and illustrations, I dedicate this version
to all who made this happen.
—J.L.

ISBN 978-0-545-48570-8

Text copyright © 1985, 2012 by Mike Thaler
Illustrations copyright © 2012 by Jared D. Lee Studio, Inc.

Originally published as *Cream of Creature from the School Cafeteria*,
© Avon Camelot, October 1985

12 11 10 9 8 7 6 5 4 3 2 1   12 13 14 15 16 17/0

Printed in the U.S.A.   40

First Scholastic printing, September 2012

It was lunchtime.

Our class walked slowly toward the cafeteria, holding our noses.

We could smell the food all the way
down the hall.
It was also making funny noises.
We opened the cafeteria door.

We took our trays
and were about to line up . . .
when we backed away
from the lunch counter in horror!

The meatloaf was moving!!
It wiggled and jiggled in the pan.

Then it slurped out of the pan,
slid off the counter, and slithered
across the cafeteria floor.
It was coming at us!!!

We threw our lunch trays in the
air and ran out the door!

Mrs. Crumb, the cook, ran out of the cafeteria, shouting at the meatloaf. She tried to hit it with a serving spoon.

The loaf blurped over her shoes,
and she was gone!

We ran into the main office.
"Call the sheriff!" we all shouted.
"Now, what's wrong?"
said Mrs. Bagley, the principal.
She smiled.

"The meatloaf is after us!"
we screamed.
"Now, now," smiled Mrs. Bagley,
opening the office door and
stepping out.
"There's absolutely nothing to—"

GLURP!

She never finished
her sentence—
she just disappeared
into the burbling loaf.

We ran into her office and locked the door.
Through the glass we could see the meatloaf eating all the safety posters.

We dialed the sheriff.
Soon we heard his siren.

He burst in, took out his badge,
and told the loaf not to move.
The food moved . . . then chased
the sheriff all the way out of
the school.

We dialed the fire department.
A big red engine roared up.
The meatloaf was eating the flagpole.
The firemen unrolled a huge hose
and squirted the loaf with water.

The meatloaf splashed merrily
and took a bath.

We dialed the army.
A jeep pulled up.
Four soldiers jumped out with
flamethrowers.
They turned the flames on the food.

The meatloaf warmed up, it blurbbled
over their boots,
and they were all eaten
by a *hot lunch*!

We dialed the air force.
Soon two jet planes roared overhead.

They each dropped a bomb on the food, but the meatloaf just . . .

BURPED!

Then it ate the jungle gym, the slides, and all our swings.
We all screamed!

Then we thought of Mickey.
"Mickey is the only one who can save us.
Mickey will eat anything!"

We found Mickey licking the
snack machine.
We told him what had happened.
He smiled.

He walked calmly to the
center of the playground.
He sat down in front of the food—
and took out two spoons.

The meatloaf gurgled—
out came Mrs. Crumb.

The meatloaf burbled—
out came Mrs. Bagley.
The meatloaf burbled—
out flew the safety posters
and the soldiers.

The meatloaf looked at Mickey.
Mickey looked at the meatloaf.
It burbled and glurped and slithered
toward him.

CLOSER!

CLOSER!!

CLOSER!!!

Mickey's spoons flashed in the
sunlight, and . . .

HE ATE IT!
HE ATE IT ALL!!
HE ATE IT ALL UP!!!

Then he licked his spoons, twirled them, put them back in his pockets, and asked for seconds.

We all cheered!
The mayor came.

He gave Mickey a bright medal
for saving the school.

Mickey looked at the medal,
smiled . . .

. . . and ate it.